Ballet Kitty

Ballet Class

For Judith K., with love and thanks,
Bernette Ford

For little dancers everywhere,
Sam Williams

First published in Great Britain in 2008 by Boxer Books Limited.

ISBN-13: 978-0-545-20460-6
ISBN-10: 0-545-20460-7

12 11 10 9 8 7 6 5   12 13 14/0

Printed in the U.S.A.   40

First Scholastic printing, September 2009

Ballet Kitty
Ballet Class

Bernette Ford and Sam Williams

SCHOLASTIC INC.
New York Toronto London Auckland Sydney
Mexico City New Delhi Hong Kong Buenos Aires

Ballet Kitty woke up as happy as happy can be.

Her ears were pink. Her nose was pink.

And she was smiling from ear to little pink ear.

She put on her favorite pink tights and leotard,

and her new tutu and pink ballet slippers.

Today was the first day of real ballet class.

How could she wait until it was time to go?

Kitty's best friend Pussycat was

waiting outside with Ginger Tom.

Princess Pussycat had on her lilac slippers,

her lilac princess gown and cape, and of course,

her lilac jeweled crown.

Tom was wearing black shorts and a white t-shirt, but he had sneakers on his big feet.

"You can't dance in THOSE!"
said Ballet Kitty, as the three
friends arrived outside Ballet School.

"You'll trip," said Ballet Kitty.

"You'll slip," said Princess Pussycat.

"And you'll squeak," added Kitty.

"I don't care," said Ginger Tom. "I don't
want to go to ballet class, anyway!
And I WON'T wear my silly ballet shoes!"

Mademoiselle Felicity clapped her hands
and the children formed a circle.

Ballet Kitty and
Princess Pussycat
watched their teacher
and did everything

she did to warm up.

They stretched their legs.

They pointed their toes.

They raised their
arms, and shook
their hands.

But Ginger Tom was having trouble.

He couldn't stretch out his legs.

He couldn't point his toes.

When he tried to raise his arms and

stretch his hands up to the ceiling,

he fell over backward!

Princess Pussycat tried to hide a giggle.

Ballet Kitty helped him up.

Mademoiselle clapped her hands again.

Lovely piano music tinkled all around them.

Ginger Tom did much better when they all stood side by side and held the barre.

Mademoiselle showed them what to do as she called out the names of each ballet movement.

They all tried . . .

First Position

Second Position

Third Position

Fourth Position

Fifth Position

Tendu

Attitude

Plié

Curtsy

Bow

Now the ballet class moved to the

center of the floor.

The music grew louder . . . and faster!

Ballet Kitty and Princess Pussycat held hands.

Mademoiselle Felicity took Ginger Tom's hand.

Then they followed Mademoiselle
around the room in time to the music.

They walked . . .   and skipped . . .

and ran.

Ballet Kitty had never been so happy.

Princess Pussycat had to work hard,

but she loved dancing with Ballet Kitty.

As for Ginger Tom,

he did not trip.

He did not slip.

And even though his sneakers

squeaked on the shiny wood floor,

the music carried him around the room.

Ginger Tom could dance!

When the music stopped, Ballet Kitty

performed her prettiest pirouette.

Princess Pussycat curtsied.

And Ginger Tom
bent over in
a perfect bow.

There was lemonade and crackers and cheese

at Ballet Kitty's house after ballet class.

"I can't wait till next time," said Kitty.

"Me, too," said Pussycat.

"Me, three!" said Tom, and he held up his new ballet shoes. "And I think next time, I'll try these out!"